NAVITAS

BARATHRUM SERIES

LUCINDA PEBRE

For my Rebel.

CONTENTS

1

───────

Jordan looks down. A wave of dizziness washes over him, causing his fingers to tighten on the plastic drainpipe. His eyes shoot to an unremarkable spot on the brick wall inches from his nose. It's dark but he knows there's a holly bush below. There's no way he'd survive the drop.

A beam of light singles out a black wheelie bin as if it's a precious work of art; the effect ruined by the way it's parked in the middle of a spiky bush. It's not a stable landing pad even wedged there, but it's all he has.

Now that it's too late, Jordan realises that climbing out of the window was a stupid idea. He isn't strong or sporty, which has never bothered him until tonight when athletic skills might mean the difference between hanging on and dying from a fall.

Usually, he sneaks out the front door unnoticed but hadn't fancied his chances after being grounded for skipping education for the third time this week. Not wanting to walk past staff in case they try to stop him because then, the only option is to kick off like Mathew Evans. The difference is, Matt gets away with stuff because he doesn't care and no matter what staff say, they don't want to deal with his brand of trouble.

Rap music blasts from above, making Jordan flinch. He groans, recognising Skepta, Matt's favourite band. It's been on a loop in the kid's home for weeks until Jordan can't remember hearing anything else. He shakes his head, thinking at least his dangerous climb now has an appropriate soundtrack.

The world becomes surreal in a familiar way. Jordan tells himself that everything will be okay and there's no need to get stressed. He takes deep breaths like he's watched on a YouTube video dealing with panic attacks. It doesn't work, and he isn't surprised when a silvery sheen gathers in waves in front of him. Brighter strands weave through the centre; the whole mass is forever moving. He's drawn to the spectacle, but what does it mean, seeing stuff nobody else can?

"Not helping," he whispers to the light.

It's his fault. If he hadn't broken the never look down rule, he really would have been fine. There's no getting away from the fact that he's a rule-breaker and blames it on there being so many of them. According to his social worker, it's why he doesn't have a family of his own.

"If only you would listen more and not upset people so much. Janet really wanted you to stay but feels she can't keep you safe if you don't do anything she says."

When he's tempted to look down yet again, he concedes that she might have a point. Perhaps things will be different when he's old enough to be in charge of his own life. Then, he can choose to live somewhere without stupid rules, made up for the sake of it. That way, he won't be tempted to break the sensible ones, such as, not climbing out of the upper window or when he does, he won't be tempted to look down. Come to think of it, that might not be an official rule.

If he had any sense, he'd return the way he'd come and call the whole evening off. That's not what he'll do, because like it states in his EHC plan, Jordan is incapable of logical reasoning.

The hallucination has just started to fade when from under his right trainer, part of the windowsill crumbles. Rubble falls in a powdery shower, and he almost looks down again. He immediately shifts his weight, bringing his right leg parallel to the other, so both feet are against the bricks. Fortunately, the drainpipe he's straddling is sturdy, which is good since it's holding his entire weight. He remembers climbing another in a different place and time — no thinking about that, especially now.

He's okay, everything is fine. This time he must be more convincing because the light continues to fade. He's back in control and that's essential because at this stage, the trick is to take the climb slowly. Experience of other times, ones he isn't allowed to remember, tells him that if he even thinks about getting it over with, he risks gaining momentum. Then there's only one way to go — crashing down fast.

It's not right that he takes comfort in the mass of paperwork staff would have to fill in on discovering his broken body. Weirdly, he'd be remembered that way. The details recorded in some dusty basement. He doesn't know what happens to all the records written about him. Some are more accurate than others, but it all seems like a waste of time to Jordan.

His arms start to shake. At the same time, sweat forms on his forehead despite the chill in the air and both palms are becoming slick. He's not even reached the office window, otherwise known as the tricky bit. Inching down, he forces his body to take it slow even though it's harder that way. There a tremor in his tired leg muscles along with a growing temptation to go faster and get it over.

A sudden grating noise from above, followed by music blasting out makes Jordan jerk and his left foot slips. Thank God his weight is on the right else he'd have been a goner. Loud sniggering comes from overhead.

"Hey, buddy, why don't you use the front door like everyone else?"

Jordan recognises Matt's rasp. A product of daily cigarettes and cannabis consumption. With any luck, he'll move onto heroin and disappear into his room for weeks on end. That's what happened to the kid across from Jordan. Alex might still be in there for all Jordan knows. The staff couldn't or wouldn't tell them what happened, or where Alex ended up. They say it's essential to maintain confidentiality but that's bullshit. They don't bother about confidentiality when it comes to telling the other kids how Jordan doesn't see his family when he could.

Now, to add to Jordan's woes, it has started to drizzle. The rain quickly coats the plastic pipe, making it slippery and difficult to hold. Again, he tells himself that he's fine and tries hard to make it true.

At least the ground is closer now, and he's reached the tricky part. He will have to use every skill he possesses not to be spotted by the eagle-eyed staff.

There's a new one on tonight, she seems okay but as Matt says they're all nice at first. The kids know not to be taken in by a smile and occasional praise. Staff induction takes a whole month and it's only at the end they display their real character. He can see why the ones who stay are forced to become as bad as the rest. If they don't, they find themselves with bad shifts and ostracised. It means that as far as Jordan is concerned, nobody can be trusted.

The residence meetings and incentives don't fool anyone; the law of the jungle applies. Speaking of monkeys...wait, is that a logical thought? What do educational psychologists know anyway? No logical thought processes indeed.

Jordan swings his right foot so it lands on the rim of concrete that runs along the top of the window. The ridge probably has a name. Perhaps, he should go to his educational programme more often. No, he's never learnt anything from those boring lessons.

Noise drifts down from above; he had better hurry. Matt won't tell the staff about his antics. No kid, no matter their status, survives if they snitch, but it won't be long before Matt starts throwing things.

Something cold and wet lands on the top of his head. The sound of loud giggling drifts down. Jordan resists the urge to look up and see what else is about to drop on his unprotected head. Any reaction will add to Matt's satisfaction. What the bully really wants is a blurred photo to stick on Facebook with a witty caption.

Liquid with the consistency of treacle plops onto his shoulder, accompanied by a strong smell of strawberries. Milkshake perhaps? That's not so bad, but it is going to get worse.

Jordan is almost there. If he falls now the paperwork will be just as bad, but he'll survive, perhaps with a broken bone or two.

Above, it's gone quiet. Either Matt has gone to fetch

another one of his cronies, or he's in the office. Jordan hopes it not the latter because Matt will find some way of making trouble.

Taking a deep breath, Jordan angles his body as much as possible and jumps. He is aiming for the wheelie bin. Both feet hit the top at an angle, causing the whole thing to topple backwards, throwing him into the holly bush — foul-smelling bags of rubbish spill out on top of him. Fortunately, a thick coat and jeans protect most of his body, but his hands and face suffer minor scratches that wouldn't be worth the paperwork.

Jordan doesn't move for a few seconds, waiting to see if anyone has heard the noise and is coming to investigate. His shoulders slump at the sound of Evan's hyena laugh, and he closes his eyes. When he opens them again, he's still stuck in the bush but at least he's alive.

2

____

White teeth gleam in the light cast by an electric fire. Canines that are way too long to belong to anyone human. Sapphire thinks that with his bloodshot eyes, he could star in a horror movie, as long as vampires were the main feature.

She stares up at the blood sucker, who is the embodiment of her nightmares. "Holy mother of God, save us."

Feminine laughter drifts from the far side of the room; a woman amused by a harmless joke. Sapphire doesn't expect anything else from her mother.

The words slip out before Sapphire can clamp her jaw together. "You evil cock sucking witch."

The vampire pauses, glancing over his shoulder. "Hell Madison, you didn't warn me she had a mouth like a toilet."

"I know, darling. Real, religious nut-jobs just don't use language like that."

Sapphire bristles at the insinuation that she's not devoted to God. She's about to argue but recognises the reason for her irritation. It's too close to the truth. Hasn't she learned it's best not to speak? Not to give Madison any ammunition.

The demon has gone from full vamp into, *let me have a sip of brandy before the torture begins*. Both eyes revert to normal and his canines are gone. This is her best chance.

"Sapphire, don't you dare." Her mother always anticipates what she's going to do next.

Sapphire suspects it's nothing to do with magic, although if so, it's the only thing Madison doesn't use magic for. Tasks from brushing hair to cooking toast all need to be enhanced in Madison's world.

Sapphire consoles herself that so far, she has stayed strong and not allowed temptation to get the better of her. At least, not since Father Gerrard set her straight. She isn't Roman Catholic but when he came to the school to talk about...she can't remember what...some charity thing. That's when her life changed for good.

Back then, Sapphire didn't know what gave her the courage to stay behind and speak to him. Perhaps he looked as if he was going to say something funny even though he never did.

She remembers, Tommy Banks telling her not to do it. He said priests liked little girls too much, but she didn't believe him. Tommy was always full of shit. Afterwards, he told everyone she was not a virgin. It didn't bother her, mainly because it was a long time before she knew what he meant and by then, she was consumed with too many earth-shattering worries to care about his lies.

"Father."

Is that what you call a priest? She was not sure because her only guide was from movies. As soon as the words were out, she was sure it was a mistake.

The man's pale blue eyes fastened on her in a way that made her believe he saw her soul. Inside she curled up, trying to protect her secret self. The part that she didn't want anyone to see.

"Would you like to tell me something?" There was a gleam in those washed out eyes, an eagerness that made Sapphire shuffle back. "It's okay, I will not judge. Only God can judge."

His words offered little reassurance because he might as well be God. It was too late to back down, she had to give him something and her mind wasn't practiced enough to make up a convincing lie.

A familiar buzzing started inside her head, like a million flies rising off a carcass. The magic stirred within, sensing distress and wanting to help. She pushed it down, refusing to let it out. She was not allowed to show it at school.

It was only by looking away from his eyes and down at her feet that she could answer. "It's more a question." Both shoes were splattered with dry mud from the puddle outside the main entrance. "Does God know everything?" She resisted the urge to rub the top of one shoe on the back of her long socks.

He let out a sigh, full of disappointment. "Is that your question?"

"No," she said immediately, because she hoped that this man could help. "I want to know where magic comes from."

He made a strangled noise, followed by silence, which was long enough for her to regret blurting out the question. "You are too young to be tainted by magic."

She couldn't speak and stared hard at the door wanting to yank it open and escape. Outside of her family, adults never admitted the existence of magic. Impossibly, the distance to the door had grown, not that it mattered because her feet were rooted to the spot and she could no more take one step than she could circumvent the globe.

"No, maybe you are not." The words were spoken softly as if not intended for her. "The trouble with magic is that it comes from the devil and by using it, you condemn your soul for all eternity. Is your soul black, little girl?"

She tried to open her mouth but her jaw felt wired shut. Only now, she noticed that the mud wasn't confined to her shoes, it was on her socks as well. It was a weird thing to care about at a time like this.

Sapphire has no idea what would have happened if Mr Beresford hadn't stumbled through the door with an armful of text books. She remembered that he wasn't at all apologetic and it occurs to her that he might have done it on purpose.

Sapphire has never told Madison why she refuses to use magic, or about her decision not to blacken her soul any further. She would trust God to help her be strong and to resist the evil in her own house.

The vampire moves closer. "There's power in her blood." He sniffs the air. "It calls me."

Ice clinks against glass. "I told you earlier, take a sip, unless you're worried you won't be able to stop. She's no use to me as she is."

The vampire shifts to the left, allowing Sapphire to see her mother for the first time tonight. Madison sways, a crystal glass dangling from one hand. There's an inch of clear liquid in the base that isn't water.

"This is your fault, dear."

Sapphire gasps. "How?"

"You could stop him, if you want."

Sapphire wonders how much her mother has had to drink and whether the alcohol is impairing her judgement. If so, this situation could turn bad. The vampire might take things too far and then none of Sapphire's prayers will help her survive until morning. Even then, she will not use magic.

"Our father who art in heaven..."

3

———

Sapphire blinks her eyes open. She's still alive! That bloodsucker didn't drain her after all, but he was going to. She'd been certain that she'd never wake.

She rubs her eyes, only to find her knuckles are wet. She can't take much more of this. The temptation to use magic is getting stronger and even though it means damming her soul, she just might do it in a fit of rage. The devil in her head laughs, wanting her to let out all the pain, direct it at a deserving target. Except, she will be the loser in the end.

The devil tells her over and over that it's okay to surrender, and then everything will be fine. Madison will behave like a mother again and not some demented evil thing. Sapphire has always known that Madison cares more about what her daughter can do than who she is. To the point where the woman is willing to subject her to torture to get what she wants. There's also the pesky fact that she would be giving up eternal life. This is a test, that's all. Oh, Saint Thomas, why is she crying again?

It's only when she tries to move that she becomes aware

of the ache in every cell of her body. She's tempted to stay in bed and skip school for once, but at least school is safe and predictable. If she stays here, anything can happen.

She forces herself out up and to the bathroom, blanching at how pale she is in the mirror. She picks at the raw scab on the side of her neck. Eventually, they really are going to kill her if she doesn't do something soon, before she's too weak to act. Already, her head is like cotton wool as she struggles to remember today's classes.

With a deep breath, she goes downstairs, almost falling and having to catch herself on the bannister. Her rucksack slides forward off her shoulder, dragging her towards the ground.

Madison sits, sipping coffee in the kitchen while reading the local paper. "Morning, darling. I'm glad to see you, I thought it would take you longer to recover." She looks up. "I've already let the school know you won't be in."

Sapphire doesn't bother arguing. She doesn't have the strength. It's going to take everything she's got to get out the front door. She grabs a slice of toast and takes a bite while heading out. The food sticks in her throat and makes her realise how thirsty she is, but a drink will take too long. Never mind that there is no way she can swallow the cloggy mess without one.

Madison says, "Don't think about leaving, if you do, I'll send Dalton after you."

Sapphire can't hide the revulsion that takes hold as she tries in vain to suppress a shudder. There's no need to ask who Dalton is even if she didn't get his name last night. After everything, she still struggles to believe that her own mother can do this.

Madison's eyes soften. "You might not believe me, but

I'm sorry it's come to this. You can stop all this nonsense by just using your power." She places the paper on the table, amongst the cereal dishes and marmalade jar. "This refusal to embrace who you are has gone on long enough."

Sapphire's extremities tingle, warning her of danger. If she doesn't move soon, she won't be able to and it'll be game over.

"Why don't you sit down and have a decent breakfast?"

The words, like so many, sound reasonable, and Sapphire has to fight the part that wants to believe them. It'd be so easy to give in, but then her life would be over. She would belong to the coven to use as they wanted.

With Madison's words ringing in her ears, *it's for your own good,* Sapphire races down the stone steps. Her head is swimming, making it doubly hard to pay attention to her surroundings.

Somehow, she makes it to the street where a bus stops in front of her, and she clambers aboard without checking the destination. She flashes her pass at the driver who doesn't bother to look and slumps in the disabled seat at the same time as the bus lurches forward. At the end of the street, they turn left instead of going straight on. She barely notices because her head is getting worse, and she is leaning over her knees trying not to retch.

Someone pats her shoulder. Sapphire raises her head to meet the brown eyes of a white-haired old lady who smiles and presses a hand to her forehead.

"No fever." Her voice is thin and weak. "Pregnant?"

Sapphire tries to shake her head but stops as soon as she starts, feeling acid bubble in her trachea.

The woman shuffles towards the exit. "Course not."

She chuckles, suddenly sounding younger and stepping

out onto a busy street that Sapphire doesn't recognise. In fact, she doesn't know this part of the city at all. Before she can panic, she remembers that most buses end up at the central bus station at some point. All she has to do is stay on and wait.

Her breathing starts to come easier. That's better. What's happening? She realises that this is more than blood loss. The coven must have done something to make her ill, and it's only by chance that she's gone the wrong way. Maybe God is looking out for her. With a bit more luck, it'll take time for them to find her again and hopefully by then she'll be far away. She curses herself, she should have known that Madison wouldn't let her go so easily.

She's alone, with very little money and no plan. School's out because that's the first place they will look. Panic threatens to drive her back into a sorry state.

First things first, she needs to get out of her school uniform. That way, she won't have a problem with people thinking she's skiving.

Sapphire's bag is always packed ready, and it helps that there are only a couple of passengers who are in their individual electronic worlds. They don't pay her any attention as she stumbles to the back where she changes clothes, one piece at a time.

Despite the lack of planning, and with horror stories of what happens to young women on the streets circling in her head, Sapphire starts to think she has a chance. If she doesn't know where she's going, nobody else can either.

4

Jordan waits in the shadow of a doorway directly across from the library's main entrance. Keys weigh down the right pocket of his jeans. In his left, he fingers a disc. The action helping him stay calm. Heat from his hand warms the metal as he turns it over and over, needing reassurance that it's still there. It's all he has from his former life, and he takes it everywhere since nothing is safe in the home. He doesn't need to look at it anymore, the engraving of an eagle surrounded by a circle is seared in his mind.

If anyone notices him, they don't pay any attention. It's too cold to linger, but he has to make sure the librarians have gone. A couple of weeks ago, he'd stumbled into one going home. The librarian had peered at him suspiciously before he veered towards the bus station. A few seconds later and it would have been obvious he was planning to break into the building.

The dull light in the entranceway is on but that doesn't mean anything, sometimes they leave it on overnight. At this time of year, it's dark when they arrive for work in the morning. Still, there's no sign of life and the main door has been locked for over an hour.

Once the street is empty, Jordan slips down a narrow passage to a side door. Off the Main Street it's easy to unlock without being seen. As soon as he's inside, he lets out a breath, the tension leaving his shoulders. Even though he's here illegally, entering the library is almost a religious experience. There's something about the smell of dry paper, dust and ink; of being surrounded by a vast amount of knowledge that makes him feel as if he's in the presence of something greater than himself.

Light that only he can see drifts into view. It's always present here, adding to Jordan's conviction that there's something special about this place. For a minute, he stares at a silver-plated picture frame, fascinated by the colours reflected back by the ethereal light. He makes his way down the corridor as quietly as possible. There's nothing he can do to stop his feet clicking on the floor. Well, he could take his shoes off and in summer he does, but with the temperature expected to drop below freezing tonight, the tiles will be too cold through his thin socks.

Nothing is out of place and everything's the same as usual, which is why he can't work out why he has a niggling worry that he's not alone. Ribbons of luminescence become increasingly wavy the further he goes. A faint shuffling noise comes from his right, inside the reference section.

Wild images of blood and dark entities fill his head. Jordan fights the memories. There's a reason he doesn't talk about his past even though it's a major issue for social workers. A member of staff once recorded that Jordan doesn't remember his family. It isn't true; he tries not to remember, there is a difference. Talking about his life would inevitably lead to questions about the night his mother died. How can he explain the presence of demons and vampires? They would think he was even more of a weirdo than they already do. One thing's for sure; he should have died, not his mother. So, it's not surprising that his imagination conjures the worst.

He can almost hear her telling him to be careful, as he pauses in the aisle where most books can only be carried one at a time due to their size. He's not sure what to do; most of him wants to run away but then he won't ever know, and his safe place will have become dangerous. No, he has to check out the noise even though he doesn't want to. Now, he wishes he'd removed his shoes, but daren't take the time.

Moving slowly, he follows the shiny ribbons, hoping they aren't leading him into a death trap. The only light comes from the radiant strips, but it's enough for him to see his way between the enormous bookcases. Until he knows what he's dealing with, he cannot come up with a plan and has to wing it. Whenever he's done that in the past, things haven't gone well. All he can do is take his time and hope for the best.

Fortunately, the light is happy to go at his pace. Although, when he comes to turn a corner, there's no way of checking what he's going to find. With a deep breath, he sticks his head around first, his body only following when the way is clear. After three uneventful manoeuvres, he becomes complacent and on the fourth turn almost walks straight into a girl.

She gasps, at the same time as he squeaks. They stare at each other in disbelief until Jordan recovers his wits. This girl is no scary demon but she is in his secret place — an intruder spoiling his sanctuary.

"What are you doing here?" He frowns. "How did you get into the building?"

It's hard to see any detail in the dark, but she can't be much older than him unless she's short for her age. In Jordan's limited experience, girls always look and act older.

She crosses her arms, scowling back without any sign of fear. "I don't owe you an explanation. You don't own this place any more than me."

Jordan shakes his head, thinking that much is obvious. "I have a key." It's one he stole, but he doesn't have to tell her everything.

She narrows her eyes. "A key. So, if we ring the police, you will be able to explain the reason for your late-night visit?"

Jordan's shoulders slump, he can tell by the way she cocks her head to the side that she's fully aware that he doesn't want the police involved. "You aren't meant to be here either," he mutters under his breath.

"I was just..." she can't seem to find the right words, "reading and lost track of time."

That's not remotely believable but Jordan sees an opportunity. "So, you're looking for the way out? I can help with that."

"Oh yes, with your key." She looks down at the ground between her feet. "The truth is, I haven't anywhere to go." She scuffs a shoe across the floor. "I might have hidden under one of the bookshelves at closing time."

"Don't be silly; there's no way you would fit under there." Jordan points to the space at the base of the bookcase even though it's too dark to see."

"Not that one. There's room back there, where two shelves don't join properly."

Jordan shakes his head. She's probably telling the truth but he is torn. He doesn't want to share his sanctuary but can't throw her out if she really doesn't have anywhere to go. Unlike a lot of thirteen-year-olds, he hasn't been sheltered from reality and knows there are reasons why someone might not have any place to go. The ribbons of light are congregating around her, giving her a white aura. Of course, she cannot see what's happening, but it's a sign that he should help her.

He reluctantly holds out a hand. "I'm Jordan."

It takes her a couple of seconds to respond and when she takes his hand, her grip is firm. "Sapphire."

"What sort of name's that?" The words fall out.

She snatches her hand back and snaps, "I don't like it but there's not much I can do, is there?"

He instantly regrets the slip. "Sorry." It's obvious she shared her real name, and she didn't have to. Wanting to make it up to her, he says, "I know where we can get a hot drink. There might even be biscuits."

She sags a little and nods, not going as far as to smile. The uncanny light congregates around her, illuminating her face.

Jordan leads the way to the tiny staff kitchen off the main corridor. She follows him with both hands held out in front of her like a mummy. He's surprised she can't see with all the light surrounding her.

Sapphire jumps as he clicks on a reading lamp. She looks around at the sudden brightness as if sure someone is about to nab them.

Jordan points to the skylight window. "It's okay, nobody

can see in here. This room is on the opposite side of the building to the street, and there's no security because people don't rob books."

Now there's time to look, Jordan sees that she's younger than he first thought. Her face is pale, and there are dark smudges under her eyes as if she hasn't slept in a long time. He feels an unexpected affinity with her, even though he doubts her experiences have been anything like his.

5

The last few hours merge into a blur. Sapphire now thinks escaping home was the easy part and the real challenge is going to be remaining free. She remembers her mother's threat to send Dalton after her and shudders. Not wanting to think about it, but knowing Madison isn't going to let her go, it occurs to her that search party is likely to be made up of both the coven and vampire. She can't ask for help from anybody she knows because that will be the first place they will look.

She had come to the library by accident, searching for somewhere to gather her wits and get warm. After that, everything has happened so quickly, there hasn't been time to make plans or overthink the danger. It was only when she sat down that it hit her and by then her brain wasn't functioning too well. That's why curling up in the tiny space between bookcases had been all she could do, despite the devil in her head describing other possibilities.

There's no way she's going to tell Jordan, but she's grateful for his appearance because it's distracted her from the devil's temptation. By pretending everything's normal for him, it helps her to believe the world is the way it is on the surface, not full of evil.

Thank you, God, for leading me to safety. She barely resists adding that striking the vampire down would have worked out even better. What is wrong with her? She shouldn't be having such thoughts.

Jordan smiles in triumph, brandishing a packet of Coop own brand chocolate biscuits. "We'll only be able to have a couple each. I don't want anyone to get suspicious."

He fills the kettle, going straight to the cupboard to retrieve two mugs. He knows which drawer the spoons are in. Sapphire realises this is routine for him, he really does come here regularly. Don't his parents miss him? If she asks, she's worried it'll encourage return questions that she's not ready to answer. Instead, she perches on the edge of a hard-wooden chair and takes a biscuit between her fingers.

She nibbles along an edge. "Which is your favourite section?"

It's an inoffensive question, but Jordan freezes as if she's requested his bank details. "What?"

Thinking he might have misunderstood, she adds, "What do you like to read?"

With exaggerated slowness, he turns to face the kettle. "I don't read." When she doesn't say anything, he adds, "I can read, but it's difficult to concentrate." He blurts, "I have ADHD."

There's a boy in her class with ADHD, so she has some idea of the condition, but that isn't the bit that makes no sense. "Why do you hang out in a library then?"

"I like being around books." Without looking at her, he gestures to the packets and jars next to the sink.

"Tea, one sugar, please." Then, because he still doesn't look at her, she says, "Sorry, I didn't mean anything by it."

"It's okay, everyone thinks I'm a freak."

She laughs and when he stiffens again, hurriedly says, "That's what people call me..." she trails off, not sure how to continue without revealing too much.

Jordan gives her a purple owl mug before retreating to a stool near the sink as if afraid to get too close. Both hands are curled around his own plain white cup as he scrunches in on himself. The posture reminds her of the homeless guys she passed outside on her way here. They looked as if they were trying to conserve body heat while sitting or lying outside for hours and hours, whereas Jordan seems too clean to be living on the streets and surely, he's too young. Their ages cannot be far apart.

It occurs to her that she is homeless now and her eyes burn. God will take care of her. All of this is a test of her faith, and she's already passed everything else life has thrown at her without resorting to magic. What's one more trial before things get better?

She takes a sip of tea to distract herself from feeling sorry for herself. "It's good, just the right strength and sweetness." The liquid is too hot but she forces the drink down anyway. "Most people are stingy when adding sugar as if half a spoon is the same as a full spoon." She's rambling. The skin on her arms prickle and she almost drops the mug. "Did you hear something?"

Jordan is staring at the door, his drink discarded on a nearby shelf like he senses it too. He lifts his head, looking for all the world as if he is sniffing the air.

He stands. "Something is here."

Something, the word sends ice down her spine. With nowhere else to put it, she sets her mug on the Lino.

"Take your shoes off," he whispers.

She doesn't question the order, too confused by what's happening to argue. Slipping off her trainers, she shoves them in her bag where they stick out of the top. The floor is cold but she hardly notices.

If it's the vampire, he will find them through their heartbeat; and if it's Madison, she'll have some unique way of tracking them. No, this isn't about Jordan, they are hunting her.

"You go," she whispers. "They are after me."

Jordan stares at her for a moment as if considering the offer, before shaking his head and pointing to a door that looks like a closet. If he thinks they can hide, he is mistaken.

She feels a sudden need to shake some sense into him. He can't know what they are dealing with. The arrogant, self-centred fool, it will serve him right if the damn vampire drains all the blood and throw the dry husk of his body into some dusty cellar.

What is she thinking? God would not approve of such ungenerous thoughts. If they are going to have any chance, they need to act quickly. With no better idea, Sapphire yanks open the door, revealing pitch blackness. Not wanting to wait for her eyes to adjust, she steps inside.

The texture of the floor changes and a deeper chill seeps through her feet. It must be stone. For a moment, she wonders if she's being doubly foolish by trusting someone she's only just met. There again, he's the only chance she's got.

She inches forward, feeling for the edge of a step with her foot. With one hand on a rough brick wall for balance, her toes curl over the edge of the first and she hurries down, counting twelve.

Jordan is close behind. He flicks on a light switch, revealing a vast space with stack upon stack of books and papers. Deep shadows hide the scope of the place.

Sapphire's heart sinks as she realises the futility of what they are doing. If they were hiding from humans, this might work, but they have just trapped themselves in a basement.

6
___

Jordan has no idea who is after them, but it isn't anybody human. The luminescence is moving away up towards the cellar entrance in straight lines. It is behaving like it did the night his mother died. His mind shies away from that thought, although his reluctance to see the stuff has vanished. The more information, the better; if they are going to survive.

Sapphire's arms are wrapped tight around her body. She is taking rapid, shallow breaths and he's worried she's not going to be able to function in another minute.

"It's okay," he risks whispering. "There's another way out. It's just I don't have a key for down here."

He's not sure the words mean anything to her and decides it's best to show her. It takes a few minutes to pick their way through the haphazard stacks that appear to have been dumped without order or system.

They reach the back where there's a false wall, which only goes halfway to the ceiling. It runs the full width of the room, and there's no entrance, just crumbling bricks. When

Sapphire just stares at him, Jordan gestures for her to put a foot in his hand. With something that looks like despair in her eyes, she does as he gestures and he hoists her so she can reach the top. She hauls herself up until she's straddling the wall and stares down at the other side with wide eyes.

Jordan tries to find something reassuring to say but can't think of anything. There are fewer ribbons of light and he's afraid that something is sucking them up. With that to spur him on, Jordan throws himself at the wall and manages to climb partway. He teeters, not quite able to manage the last bit. His face burns at the thought of Sapphire watching. Before he falls back, she grabs his arm and drags him up the last couple of feet.

She's surprisingly strong. When Jordan chances a glance at her, he's relieved to see that she's too distracted by the sight on the other side to judge his lack of prowess.

Jordan jumps down on top of a table and is reminded of the wheelie bin incident when he skids off the lacquered edge. At least there's no rubbish to cover him and add to his embarrassment.

There aren't any books in this section, and as it's further from the bulb, the shadows are deeper. There's a change in the structure of the building. Smaller bricks that are darker with uneven cement make this part of the building look older, even to Jordan's untrained eyes.

He has often wondered if the library staff know what's stored in here because the dust lies thick and undisturbed. It is possible that they are too caught up in the daily routine to investigate all sections of the library. It is an enormous building, after all.

He scans the area. To him, it looks like a load of ancient

furniture, but he has no idea where it came from or why it's here. There's even a full set of armour and swords.

Sapphire drops onto an uncovered chaise lounge, which is a much better choice than the table. Plumes of dust shoot up as she lands, forcing her to cover her nose and mouth to stop a sneeze. The less noise they make, the better, although Jordan has a nagging feeling that it's too late.

Jordan heads to a far corner, hoping he can find the grating that leads to the outside. If he's right about what's after Sapphire, they don't have much time. Best not to think about it too much else memories might catch him first.

It's been a while since he was here exploring the extent of his playground but everything is as he remembers. He moves pots and framed pictures out of the way, searching for an oak table top, which he'd left hidden. His hands become dry and itchy form the dust. There's a faint smell of damp and Jordan stifles a sneeze, pressing his face into his elbow.

Sapphire seems distracted as she picks up one of the swords. Jordan imagines she's thinking of taking a weapon to use against whatever is coming, but he knows from experience they are too heavy to be any use.

There are only a few ribbons of light left. Despite doing his best to resist the memories, they slip through his guard, and he remembers. On the night his mother died, the luminescence had gotten thin before disappearing altogether. What's happening now is similar. That's one of the reasons he's so sure that there's nothing normal about what's hunting them. In a deep part of his soul, he knows what it is, something he had hoped never to encounter again.

Jordan picks his way through bookcases and chairs to find a roll of dirty red carpet. Thankful that everything's the same as he remembers, he pushes it out of the way, almost knocking over a lamp in his eagerness. Behind, he finds the oak table top, which he rolls aside, revealing the grate.

"It's over here." He doesn't bother whispering anymore, sure they've made too much noise already and are out of time.

The grate is loose. The way he left it when he had last crawled through the opening to see where it would lead. He pulls it away from the wall to reveal a black hole.

Sapphire hesitates before coming over to join him. She still has a sword in her hand and has to lean it against an upside-down table leg. She stares into the dark hole and mutely shakes her head at the drop into a tunnel. It's the source of the damp smell, Jordan detected earlier, much stronger now.

"There's no water," he says, meaning to reassure her, "and we don't have a choice. It's the only way out without going up there." He rolls his eyes to the ceiling.

"Where does it go?"

He whispers close to her ear, breathing in a lungful of her girly scent. "Pub, down the block. Not too far."

She shakes her head again and backs away, before seeming to think about it. Then she takes a deep breath, coming close and swinging her legs over the hole. With eyes fixed on Jordan, she jumps.

7

————

Sapphire has lost her mind. There is no choice but to jump into the dark dank hole where rats and snakes make their homes. The boy, she can't help thinking of him as that, even though he must be the same age as her. He is her only hope. Surely, he has been sent by God to save her. It's the only explanation as to how she met him in a closed library when he doesn't even read. The thought makes her want to laugh at the absurdity of it all. One thing's certain, she can't refuse God's help, especially as she'll be on her own, going up against those infinitely more powerful.

Even with God on her side, her heart thunders in the narrow passageway. Now, she really feels like a rabbit. She stifles a hysterical giggle.

The walls are damp and cold. Slime squelches between her fingers and despite her belief that Jordan has been sent to help her, she cannot stop feeling guilty that she's gotten him into this. She had offered him the opportunity to leave, but there's no way he can know what they're facing.

As the floor slopes upwards, it changes and her palms gather a coating of sand on top of the slime. It's pitch-black, and she worries how she'll know when they reach their destination. Although her phone has an inbuilt torch, she daren't switch it on in case Madison has a way to track it. Best to focus on getting to the pub, not that they're guaranteed to be safe when they arrive, but at least there's a chance.

A cobweb touches her face, causing her to shake her head violently, trying to get rid of every trace of the whispery net. She has an image of emerging in the middle of a busy pub, wanting to blend in, while covered in dirt and cobwebs.

Her knuckles bump against brick, at the same time as Jordan says, "There's a latch above."

"Bloody hell. If you can see in the dark, it would have been better for you to lead the way." Then she realises that he probably sent her first to protect her from anything coming from behind. "Sorry." She should have tried harder to explain what they are up against.

It takes a couple of minutes to locate and negotiate the lock on the trap door. Once she does, she cautiously lifts it and peers through a crack to find it's almost as dark as the tunnel.

She pushes and the door crashes to the floor behind. Wincing, she's tempted to wait and see if anyone comes to investigate, but there's no point remaining vulnerable with Jordan trapped behind and unable to help if they are attacked. She scrabbles out, surprised when his hand lands on her shoulder.

"Are you out?" His voice comes from inside the tunnel where he cannot reach her.

Sapphire shrieks, throwing herself forward and landing hard on her hands and knees. "Who's there?" Adrenaline courses through her veins, making everything brighter and more vibrant.

The only sound comes from Jordan shuffling. "What is it?" He stumbles past.

Familiar laughter so close that it almost makes Sapphire lose control of her bladder. There's no doubt it's the vampire.

"Foolish humans, you think I can't track you. The smell alone is enough but then you aren't exactly quiet."

The area is suddenly flooded with light revealing the creature crouching with an arm shading his eyes. He's wearing the expensive suit from earlier, which looks so incredibly out of place in this dirty place. Sapphire has time to register that they are in a cellar, with barrels and wooden crates stacked on all sides.

She struggles to get enough air into her lungs. "What do you want?"

This is wrong. Madison is using him, but surely he knows that. Sapphire's mind works rapidly. They will never be strong enough to fight him but if she can get him on their side. Yeah, by offering what? It isn't as if she has anything, he can't take but she has to try for Jordan's sake. He doesn't deserve to die with his soul damned for all eternity, tainted by exposure to magic.

The vampire smirks at her, and she remembers that she asked a question. "What has Madison offered you?"

"No, no, no, not everything is about money or sex. You should have learnt that by now." His head swivels left, more owl-like than human. "I do this for the joy of it. Oh, and the power." He cocks his head on one side, still resembling a bird, but more like a parrot or robin now. "There's so much power in your blood."

Sapphire open's her mouth to say...what? She doesn't know what will change what's about to happen. He moves in a blur. On top of her. Fangs like knives, coming at her throat. In the split second before he tears into her pink, delicate skin, her mind rebels. Why should she die? Torn apart by a creature that has no right to exist when she has the power to stop it? All the fear and anger of the last twenty-four hours surges out in a fiery hot stream of magic.

The cellar fills with the smell of burning flesh. An unholy screech makes her clamp both hands over her ears as she struggles to get as far away from the noise as possible.

Sapphire reels, going from a certainty she's going to die, to knowing that she failed the most important test of her life. When it came to it, she just wasn't strong enough.

White light and sound, so full of pain. Pain she caused. The devil in her head dances, *pain to vampire scum. See what happens, what you can do if you try. Are you listening to me?*

Barrels shatter and beer spurts in the air, drenching them all. Not that she notices, too caught up in the horror of what she's done. How could she? Just when she was thinking about eternal damnation. How can she argue that she's innocent when it's inside, speaking to her?

Madison had laughed at her talk of her soul being tortured in the pits of hell. Better hot than cold, she'd said.

Sapphire rises, desperate for a way out, needing to get away from the sound. There's a small window. She staggers over and fights with the stiff latch, determined to leave before she is forced to deal with what she's done.

"We can get out this way."

Jordan coughs close by. "We can't run forever."

"You don't have to come with me." It's a ridiculous thing to say since staying in the cellar with an injured vampire isn't an option.

Jordan's at her shoulder. "I know, come on." He pushes the frame out, climbs through and holds out an arm.

She grabs his elbow, vaguely aware of movement behind. Jordan clasps her wrist and pulls before she's ready. Desperately, she kicks out with one foot, hitting the wall and propelling herself out.

Cold air and rain hit her all at once but she's never been more relieved. *Go back, go back and finish the job. Half a job, that's what you are. All you've done is make him angry.* The devil's voice is more insistent than ever before and she can't make it shut up.

They run around the building to the populated side. With heads down, they hope to merge with people doing their late shopping.

"We can't keep running," Jordan repeats his belief from earlier.

The words send a shiver down her spine because what alternative is there? "I'm not using magic," She says before Jordan's surprised expression reminds her that he doesn't know anything about her or magic or vampires.

It's hard to believe because of the way he's taken everything in his stride as if it's normal to be hunted in everyday life. On reflection, Jordan must know her world, even if he is human. There's no way he would be acting as if he's enjoying himself otherwise.

8

———

They race down the street, feet slapping on the wet pavement. Full of adrenaline and exhilaration at the closeness of their escape, Jordan has never felt so alive.

The hunters aren't going to give up, but he has no intention of abandoning his new friend. Sapphire trusts him, not only that but they met in his favourite place, and the way the light reacts to her. It means they have something in common. He ignores the thought that it won't matter if they are dead.

Sapphire glances over her shoulder. "Come on, doesn't ADHD make you faster?"

Jordan ignores the jibe, concentrating on not losing her. Now that he's found someone different, like him, he's curious to know if things will change. They run past the City Hall, past the fountains in the peace gardens where water runs through green channels between patches of manicured grass. Two yellow jacketed guards patrol to stop vandalism, but there's no point asking for help, not when their enemy moves unseen.

Sapphire is still in the lead and Jordan has to put on a spurt to grab her arm. Hair whips around her face and her eyes have a touch of wildness to them, but she does slow down. Her expression relaxes at the lack of apparent pursuit.

No, he thinks, she's not really like him, but maybe she sees the world in the same way. Perhaps, she gets distracted by shiny things as well. Jordan has been alone for so long, it hurts to think things could be different. He grins, she took out a vampire, which is unbelievably cool. If only he could tell Matt, the other boy would be so jealous.

His mind returns to the horror of the cellar. It's proving hard not to remember the past, and the danger is that now he's started, he won't be able to stop. Perhaps because he's repressed everything for so long, it feels as if it's waiting to burst out.

For now, Jordan maintains that if nobody knows what happened, they can't remind him and he can at least pretend to be normal. It hasn't fooled anyone so far. People see through his act, which is probably why he has so much trouble at the kids' home.

The vampire's presence triggers his suppressed memory. There's something about the way the creature moves and his sheer power that makes Jordan feel as insignificant as a rat. That's too much like the night he refuses to remember.

Is it cowardly to be afraid of the past? Matt says so, but he's never lived through anything like the worst night of Jordan's life. The night he lost his mother forever.

It took Jordan years to accept that Chantelle was gone and not coming back for him, and so different from the relief of his father's death. The night she died, he shouldn't have been at the house but she'd asked him to bring...Kassi, that was her name. The rest is a jumble of terror and confusion that he's too afraid to unpick.

Kassi was nice. He liked her even though she was different from everyone else he'd ever met. In some ways, she was like him, even though she wasn't human. With more luminescence around her than most people, it stuck to her skin giving her a translucent quality. At the time, he didn't understand much because he'd been too young. Things might have turned out different if he'd been older. His brain keeps on with unhelpful stuff like that, which is why he doesn't think about that night. Nothing can change what's already happened.

He doesn't want to think about how Kassi tried to save him. Would she help now? He remembers the way she always made time for him when nobody else did. She didn't smile often and refused to do what he wanted but there was often a sparkle of amusement in her eyes. Then on top of everything, she killed his father.

You can't keep running, the words in his head sound like his mother. It's true, but when he it earlier, Sapphire hadn't listened, but she might now.

It gives Jordan the courage to speak, even though Sapphire's silence makes it clear she doesn't want to talk. Jordan recognises that she's upset. At least she's stopped racing ahead like it's possible to outrun a bloodsucker. She's still going too fast.

Jordan's breath comes in bursts, and he does his best to ignore the pain in his side. "Sapphire, if we run, they will catch us." Not that he knows who they are.

Her green eyes flash at him. "You think I don't know that.

Do you want the same as everyone else; for me to use magic? Well, it's not happening."

Jordan stops, surprised by the venom in her voice. "I only meant —" Magic, is that what she thinks it is?

Now, she's too far ahead to hear anything he says; and he has to run to catch her rant, "That's all I've ever been. It doesn't matter that my soul is on the line, not when it's useful for everyone else. Well, it is not happening."

"No, I mean, we need to go somewhere safer." He can barely get the words out. "I know somewhere, if I can sneak you in..." How does he explain where he lives?

Whenever he mentions the kids home, people either look at him like he needs special treatment or as if it's his fault he doesn't have a family. Like he's done something to deserve where he lives. He doesn't want Sapphire to see him like that. There again, he doesn't want her to find out how much he admires her. She's the first girl he's ever really noticed and already he's in danger of developing a crush, though that might have something to do with what she did to the vampire. If she could do that again, they'd be fine. Then he realises that's what she doesn't want. To use what she calls magic.

For better or worse, he has her attention. "I live in a kids' home and hopefully, I can sneak you in." Can, not might be able to sneak you in, better to be confident.

Thank goodness, at last, she slows to a walk. "What if the...you know what, finds us there, won't it put lives at risk?"

Jordan doesn't look at her, not wanting to see her reaction. "Sure, but don't worry about it. Some of them deserve to be vampire food."

He cringes, not sure if her lack of a response is due to the word vampire or his callous attitude to his fellow house-mates. Unsure how to retract his words, he doesn't say anything.

Sapphire's voice softens, "Okay and sorry. I didn't mean to take it out on you."

Jordan lets go of some of the tension. He wants to ask her about what happened, about what she calls magic but it's obvious she's sensitive about the subject.

Whatever she did to the vampire, it wasn't some fancy self-defence move. Navitas. The word is from long ago and he can't remember who said it, but he knows it's the real name for what Sapphire calls magic.

9

———

Sapphire peeks at Jordan out of the corner of her eye. She wants to know what it's like to have nobody but can't think how to ask. Perhaps, she would have been better off without her mother and not having to run around the streets chased by vampires. There again, if she were better at putting her trust in God, she wouldn't be having such thoughts.

How far should she take that argument? Sapphire checks for signs they've been followed. She should trust that God will take care of them. Although, God might not care if they die since their souls will live on regardless. Except, she has just used magic, and therefore her soul has been recently contaminated.

Surely, she will be forgiven? Not according to Father Gerrard. It doesn't matter anyway, because she needs to do everything in her power to increase their chance of survival, just in case. In case of what? Err, this line of thinking isn't getting her anywhere. *Used your magic, stupid girl, then none of this matters.*

She scans the area. There's only the usual bunch of people in skimpy clothes, too alcohol fuelled to feel the cold. Nobody stands out as suspicious, which doesn't mean they are not being watched. They need to get off the street. Jordan's idea of going to a children's home isn't great, but she cannot think of an alternative.

A bus pulls up with brakes hissing. At Jordan's meaningful look, she hurries to climb onboard while he waits on the street as if he's going to be able to do anything against a vampire. Nevertheless, she forces a smile at his unexpected chivalry, thinking he's too young to be so polite. Grabbing the rail in the aisle, she scans the passengers for any sign of danger.

Jordan pays their fare before nudging her into a middle double seat. She complies, grateful to be next to the window where she can stare out at the bright lights in the hope of forgetting what's happening for a few seconds.

There's plenty of traffic so it can't be that late, even though it feels as if it should be morning after everything that's happened. Sapphire watches a woman in a sparkly dress as she laughs with friends outside Debenhams. Sapphire has never worn anything like that and wonders what it'd be like to dress up and go out, to be normal. Then, she notices Jordan staring at her.

There's nothing normal about Jordan. His geeky appearance hides a complex personality. It's weird how he knows about the existence of vampires. Could he be a witch or warlock or whatever, like her? No, he's too nice and helped her without needing to; everyone with power is evil, she's seen that first-hand.

Jordan looks as if he wants something, but as soon as she

turns his way, his eyes dart away. Because he's shy? This is the first time, she's studied him properly.

She clears her throat. "Why do you act like you get chased by vampires every day?"

Jordan's, head swings around to check the seats behind and see if anyone's listening. As if these people are going to take talk of vampires seriously. They'd be more interested in the best high street bargains.

At first, he doesn't say anything, giving her time to wonder if she'd imagined that he mentioned vampires earlier? Has he gone into shock at uncovering the truth?

"I'm sorry, it's just that you seemed to know. There aren't many people that's met one and lived to tell the tale. Well, not as far as I know."

"No, it's not that. It's just the question makes me remember things I'm trying hard to forget."

"You don't have to —"

"It's okay, there's too much happening to hide for much longer, and we might need what's in my head."

This isn't his problem and she shouldn't be putting him in this position, it isn't fair. "You didn't have to help me."

"I sort of did." He pauses and hesitates before saying, "It's who I am. If I didn't help and something happened to you, I couldn't live with myself. Besides, I hate vampires." She waits, knowing he'll tell her why if she's patient enough. "One killed my mother."

She gasps, because that's not what she was expecting. After everything that's happened and Jordan's reaction to events, it shouldn't be all that surprising but still, it's horrible.

He looks down. "It was a long time ago."

"That's why you live in the children's home." It slips out and she wants to kick herself for being so blunt.

Jordan doesn't seem to notice. "Yes and no. I have family, it's just that they can't cope with me. I'm hard to live with, apparently." When she doesn't interrupt, he continues in a quiet voice, "I see things." Again, he waits as if giving her a chance to stop him. "Lights that dance and swirl. Crazy, right?"

The words are said so casually that he has to be waiting for judgement, or for her to call him a liar. She wonders whether he's told anyone else.

It might help to tell him the truth and so she says, "What you see is magic and it's sent by the devil to tempt us into doing evil."

His eyes widen. "How do you know?"

She lifts her chin. "A priest told me when I was little."

He turns away and glances along the aisle, scanning faces and it makes her want to laugh. A vampire catching the bus, that would be a first. Then she goes cold, it doesn't have to be the vampire, any of the thirteen could follow them. Even her mother could be in disguise.

Her mind goes back to the old woman when she got on the wrong bus, she had been very odd. Sapphire wouldn't recognise a glamour since she had refused to learn anything about them. It would be really useful to be able to detect them now.

"I'm a witch." She isn't sure why she blurts it out except, she wants to give him something after he put himself in danger to help her. "My mother is a witch and almost everyone I know are witches."

Jordan doesn't look as surprised as he should. "And, you

believed that Priest?" His expression is intense. "That being a witch is evil?"

She tries to work out if it's disbelief in his voice. "It's not just that, I see the evil they do every single day."

"But, how do you know for sure that magic makes witches evil."

"I only know what I see." Her shoulders slump, and she frowns. "I'm not powerful enough to see magic like you?"

Jordan shakes his head and opens his mouth but instead of speaking, he scrambles off the seat. "This is our stop." He presses the bell. "I can't believe we nearly missed it." They both stumble to the doors, which whoosh open.

Jordan jumps down the steps onto the street, outside a bunch of local shops. "It's not far," he says, head going down as if anticipating a long difficult journey.

It's quiet after the noise of the bus and neither of them speak for a few hundred yards until a thought occurs to Sapphire. "Are they just going to let me inside?"

"What? No, we'll have to sneak you in, like I said earlier." He says it as if it's obvious.

Again, she's struck by how different his life is and wants to know more. "What's your favourite subject?" At his blank expression, she says, "You know, at school?"

Jordan frowns. "I don't go to school."

"Surely, you have to go to school?"

When he doesn't answer, she doesn't know what else to say. Unsure how to ask more without causing offence, since it's not any of her business. It would still be nice to know more about him.

Jordan breaks the silence, "I can't cope with school, I have enough drama at home."

She doesn't know what he means, but lets it go and they

walk in silence. They arrive, outside a large house. There's no sign announcing what it is, although she's not sure why she expected that. Of course, there wouldn't be anything so stigmatising. The building looks like a block of flats, complete with a white painted council railing going up the steps like on old people's properties.

Jordan heads for the front door. "If you slip around the back, and give me a few minutes, I'll let you in."

Sapphire waits by a pile of tab-ends, wondering if she's about to be caught since this is clearly where someone comes to smoke. They don't bother to hide the evidence, so she guesses it's staff and not the kids. It takes longer than she expects and she's freezing before the door handle rattles and the door opens a little way. Trusting that it is Jordan and not someone she needs to avoid, she slips inside.

"It was getting cold out there," she whispers.

Jordan puts a finger to his lips. "Shush."

Then, he shoves her into a cupboard. She lets him shut the door, thinking that there has to be an easier way to break-in. Inside isn't black like expected because light comes under the door, giving everything a dark grey cast. Tins and packets line the shelves, it must be a store cupboard.

She sits on the floor between a mop bucket and a box; and is just thinking about opening the door when Jordan appears. They hurry down a corridor and up some stairs. The staircase needs painting and the banister is chipped in places but other than that it could be any house. Sapphire is not sure what she was expecting but this isn't it. They're reach an upstairs landing, where a door opens, causing Jordan to curse. Sophie looks at him in surprise, not prepared for the level of vehement.

Before she can comment, a loud voice says, "Georgie, I wondered where you were sneaking off to and now, I can see." A tall muscular boy in shorts and a t-shirt steps into the corridor. "I have to say this is not what I expected. I mean a girl! We didn't know that you knew what to do with one."

Jordan doesn't respond. He's gone a deep shade of red and is staring at the floor as if waiting for it to swallow him.

Sapphire goes hot. There's a familiar out of control feeling that always accompanies her temper. In the past, it has preceded her use of magic. She's dealt with bigger, more powerful bullies and is not going to take it from some little boy.

10

———

Jordan drags Sapphire into his room, muttering, "We can't stay here, not with Matt prowling around. I wouldn't put it past him to help anybody who comes looking for us."

He paces the small space, conscious of its unhygienic state. It doesn't seem to matter that they have more important things to worry about.

"If you go, won't the social workers look for you?"

He's puzzled. "There aren't any social workers here, only staff. I haven't seen my social worker in months."

"Oh, I just assumed the staff would be social workers," She perches on the edge of his bed, "that's all." She's seems uncomfortable about the situation, and he doesn't know how to make it better.

He gestures at the bed. "You can sleep here, I'll use the chair."

She shakes her head. "There's enough room for us both on the bed."

There is, but he doesn't want to make things difficult,

especially after Matt's comments. Neither of them undress as they settle down for the night. Jordan, who finds sleep hard at the best of times, spends the night going through all the ways they might die.

In the morning, he still hasn't found a solution. He showers and dresses before Sapphire is awake. When she does stir, it's because he has decided to ask for help from the internet and his laptop is so old that the fan makes a loud whirring noise.

"Morning," she says, voice full of sleep.

"Hi."

She sits up, looking adorable with her hair stuck out at all angles. "What's the plan?"

Jordan focuses on the screen. "Nobody here gets up before noon. We are safe until then. At least, we are if this vampire is from Earth and not Barathrum."

"Barathrum?"

Jordan looks to see if she's serious but she's in the process of getting up. He can't tell if she's aware of Barathrum or not.

Sapphire locates her trainers. "Okay, but where are we going to go?" He shakes his head unable to think of anywhere feasible, and she says, "We need to keep moving."

Jordan had come to that conclusion. "We need a destination." As he says the words, something pricks the edge of his consciousness. "Someone to help us."

"I don't have anyone, but we do need to leave."

She's right and it's good to have some sort of a plan, no matter how loose. He stands. "I'll get us some food and then we can go. Sorry it's all so messed up."

"It's not your fault. You didn't have to help me. I'm just so grateful that you did because if not, I don't think I'd be here now."

Jordan looks away, his face colouring. "Come on, you can have a shower. I'll stand outside the door and keep watch. Nobody should be awake yet."

Sapphire scrambles off the bed and grabs her bag. Jordan gives her a wash bag, which he put together while she was asleep.

She takes it with a smile. "Very organised, for a boy."

Jordan positions himself at the head of the stairs where he can listen out for anyone coming from any direction. He leans against the wall, trying to think what the best thing would be to do. His mind isn't clear like other people's and he soon gives up.

It helps to pace between the stairs and the bedroom door, but every time he steps on the floor boards outside the bathroom, it creaks. He takes an extra-large stride to miss the spot, pleased when there's no noise.

His mother is in his head again, *face your fear.* It's something he hears often, but it isn't real. That might have been how she died but it wasn't how she had lived, he remembered that much.

They aren't going to be safe until they kill the vampire and send a warning to the coven. Until those wishes come true, it is best to keep moving. Why does he keep thinking that it's too late?

A door down the hall opens and Matt's tousled head appears. He bumps into the doorframe, co-ordination clearly taking a backseat this morning.

Jordan freezes, he hadn't anticipated anyone waking, and was only on the lookout for staff. He should have known that Matt would be interested in Sapphire, if only to make things difficult for him.

Matt frowns. "Is that you waking me with that creaking?" As if he doesn't already know and then, he glances to the bathroom door and grins. "Is she in there?"

Jordan moves to stand in front of the door, blocking Matt's way and also, unfortunately confirming his suspicions. He can see Matt working out how best to take advantage of the situation.

"I got up for a piss and look what I found. All sorts happening while we innocently sleep."

Matt hasn't been innocent for a long time but Jordan isn't about to argue the point. He folds his arms, very aware that he isn't at all intimidating.

Just then the bathroom door opens and Sapphire emerges, wet hair hanging to her shoulders and a ruddy complexion from the heat. She takes one look at Matt and sticks her middle finger up.

Matt laughs as she disappears into Jordan's room, letting the door bang. "Okay, spill. What are you two up to?"

"Nothing."

"There's no nothing where you're concerned, wee one. You think I don't notice? You should know better than that. Just because I don't go to school, doesn't make me dumb."

Matt moves closer and Jordan finds himself wishing Sapphire would come out of the bedroom. He has to tilt his neck as Matt gets close.

"What do you have that could interest a girl like that?" Matt glances towards the door, before stepping in so close that Jordan can smell his sleep breath and has to turn his face away. "Nope, don't see it." Matt steps back at the same time as the door opens.

Sapphire scowls at them both. "What are you doing?"

Matt points at his chest. "Me? I was offering to help a damsel in distress."

She glances at Jordan and returns her attention to Matt. "What do you know about it?"

"It's obvious you've got problems, Honey, else you wouldn't be hanging around with losers."

"I seriously doubt that you could have helped as much as Jordan has. When did you last fight a vampire?"

Jordan can't believe she's said the v-word and thinks 'fight' is pushing it. All he did was run, after Sapphire blasted the beast with her magic. If he could just get to the bedroom. With the wall at his back, he inches towards the door.

Matt laughs. "Yesterday when I played Vampyr on X-box."

"Well, that's why I'm not in your room, because you compare a paltry computer game with life and death."

Jordan coughs in surprise, not that anyone notices. Then in an effort to stop them arguing, he sounds like he's chok-ing. Ignoring the tension between Matt and Sapphire, he makes it into the bedroom. They continue their conversa-tion while he starts to gather a few things together. There isn't much. Most possessions have been lost through the multiple moves and he just cannot get passionate about clothes. Of course, he has his disc. That is always with him.

Sapphire shuts the door. "Are you nearly ready?" She comes over to look at his meagre pack. "Matt is going to meet us outside in twenty minutes."

Jordan stops and stares at her. "That's mad, we can't take him with us." At her determined expression, he says, "He doesn't believe in any of this." Under his breath, he adds, "And, he's a prick."

"I think he'll be useful."

Jordan can see that he isn't going to get anywhere by arguing. Matt probably thinks that all of this is a joke. He knew his time with Sapphire had been too good to be true.

Unable to voice further objection, Jordan asks, "Where are we going to go?"

"See that's where Matt can help. He knows of an empty house we can use. It might be a bit rough but it'll be safer than here." She pauses and swallows. "I know it seems ungrateful but Jordan, we need help and don't have many options."

Before Jordan can respond, there's a loud bang on the door. Sapphire opens it and Jordan sees Matt at the threshold. Well, at least he knocked, which is not the way he normally comes in.

Matt grins at him. "Let's go then, buddy."

Jordan sighs, as they head downstairs. There's nothing he can do about Matt, and they are desperate enough to try anything. Jordan's unconcerned about getting past staff now that Matt's with them. Elsa appears in the office doorway, clearly surprised to see them up so early.

Matt doesn't bother to try and hide Sapphire and predictably Elsa doesn't bother to question them about her. Jordan snorts to himself, that's the Matt effect.

Elsa looks towards the kitchen. "Do you want breakfast?"

Matt gives her his most charming smile. "Naw, can't you see we've things to do."

11

———

One step outside and Sapphire blinks in the sunlight escaping through a patch of grey. Anybody would think, she's been turned into a bloodsucker. Weird how the brightness gives the impression everything will be okay. Unfortunately, a dull ache at the back of her head from not enough sleep, says differently.

Matt laughs at something while Jordan scans ahead for any sign of trouble, his brow is wrinkled in concentration. She can't help appreciating how he helped her when he didn't have to. Even now when she's allowed Matt to come along, he hasn't abandoned her.

They pass a small church where most of the gravestones are so old that they lean in one direction or another. The church's heavy oak door is firmly shut. *Religion isn't going to help you stay ahead of Madison.*

Sapphire is tempted to try it anyway and probably would have if she'd been alone or just with Jordan. He would have waited patiently while she prayed, but Matt would laugh and make rude comments. She's not bothered what he thinks, but they don't need any added drama right now.

Once past the church, Sapphire's neck tingles as if someone is watching them. Even though the street is empty, anyone could be peering out from one of the houses opposite. She can't see any movement or sign that anyone's taking an interest.

They reach the shops, but the feeling hasn't lessened. People walk with purpose but nobody is waiting at the bus stop, which isn't a good sign. Neither of the boys have a clue about what time or how often the buses come. She gets the impression they are not generally out of bed until later. Matt probably due to partying, and Jordan because he spends the night at the library, doing what, she doesn't know.

"Have either of you got a phone?" Both look at her as if she's speaking a foreign language. "I'm asking," she speaks slowly, "because I daren't switch mine on to check the bus times."

"Where would we get the money for fancy phones?" Matt brandishes a small black object. "All I've got is a Nokia. No internet, see."

Jordan lets out a strangled squeak, and Matt laughs but Sapphire follows his gaze and at first, can't see anything. Something catches her eye. Close to the road, there's a shimmer in the air like an intense heat haze. She stares directly at the spot but can't make out any details.

Matt is still laughing before squinting at the same spot when his grin fades. "What the fuck is that?" He leans forward. "It's fucking Predator. You never mentioned aliens."

Sapphire tries to think of the weapons the coven uses, but her flat refusal to engage in their sinful activities means she knows very little. They need to get moving because who knows what Madison will do and even if the bus shows up right now, they can't risk the lives of other passengers. Sapphire suspects that her mother will go to great lengths to get her back, not because she wants Sapphire's power for herself but to maintain control. Madison will never allow her daughter to leave since it makes her appear weak.

Headache forgotten, Sapphire says a silent prayer for strength. For the first time in her life, she struggles to summon the energy, and the prayer feels routine and half-hearted. Right now, there are more important things to do than beg for help from a deity that has done nothing to help in the past. Horrified by her thoughts, Sapphire pushes them away. *The devil fills her mind with laughter.*

Jordan grabs her arm, pulling her back in the direction of the church and waking her to the danger they face. The only thing they can do is run. For some reason, she remembers Jordan's words, they can't run forever.

Matt catches up quickly. "I'm guessing that if that thing gets us, bad shit will happen."

Sapphire is very conscious that he's not breathing hard, whereas, neither Jordan or she have the breath to answer. They fall inside the children's home together. Matt slams the front door, leaning against it. He looks like he's back from a stroll, while Jordan and Sapphire look as if they have sprinted for miles.

Elsa sticks her head out of the office. "What are you doing back so soon? I thought you'd gone out for the day." She has the same surprised expression as earlier. "I know the buses are not so regular on a Sunday, but you didn't wait long."

Nobody answers as they head towards the stairs. Sapphire keeps her head down, hoping the woman won't notice that she doesn't live there. Only Matt appears cheerful and carefree. Sapphire wonders if Jordan's right and he doesn't believe that what's happening is real.

Elsa's eyes fasten on Sapphire. "Where are you going?"

Sapphire looks to the boys for help and when they don't respond, says the first thing that comes into her head. "I'm helping them with their homework."

Elsa's expression remains blank, but Matt grabs her left wrist and pulls her along. The woman doesn't try to stop them as they run upstairs and pile into Jordan's room.

Matt is laughing as he shakes his head. "You should have told the truth. Easier to believe in vampires than that we would be doing homework." He grins. "Don't worry, she's anything for an easy life that one. She won't bother us as long as we're quiet."

Sapphire stares at him. "You believe what I told you about vampires?"

"Hey if there are aliens, why not vampires?"

She opens her mouth to point out that there aren't any aliens and closes it. She doesn't want to get into a conversation about Madison because right now, that's beyond her. As the adrenaline starts to leave her body, her headache comes back with a vengeance. Dear God, they got away by the skin of their teeth and that thing is still out there, searching for her.

Jordan sinks to the edge of the bed. "That distortion of the air," he sounds hesitant and glances uncertainly at Matt, "light was being drawn in, like into a black hole."

Sapphire pats Jordan's arm as she sits next to him. "We wouldn't have seen it until it was too late if it hadn't been for you." Nobody sees the same as you. "Thank you and thank God."

Jordan looks down and mumbles something she doesn't catch, but she thinks he says, "It's nothing."

"Why the fuck should we thank God. It was Jordan who saw the thing. Didn't see God supplying one iota of help."

For once, Sapphire doesn't feel like arguing. Part of her thinks he's right, God doesn't help. Thanks, and prayers don't seem to change anything. When she looks up, there's a sympathy in Matt's eyes that she isn't expecting.

Jordan goes to the window and looks down at the front garden. Both hands are in his pockets, and he's hunched forward with an expression of intense concentration as if working through a math's equation.

Grateful for some distraction from the conversation with Matt, she asks, "What do you see out there, Jordon?" He doesn't move from the window but both shoulders stiffen.

Matt shakes his head. "You're a right pair of fucking freaks."

Sapphire's not expecting the laugh that bursts out of her. "I suppose we are to you, but it doesn't mean we're bad, or wrong."

Jordan relaxes a little and she realises the words make him feel better, even if she's not sure why.

Sapphire says, "I want to be friends, Jordan."

"So do I."

Matt shakes his head. "You're both nuts, as well as freaks. I should have known with a name like Sapphire, you're never going to be normal, are you?"

Sapphire stifles another urge to laugh. 'What was your first clue? Was it the talk about vampires? Or, could it have been my need to say a prayer?" She smiles at his disgusted expression.

"I get why you'd ask God for help. After all, I've done it

plenty of times myself but when I didn't get a reply, I stopped. Is he answering you, or are you just stupid? I just want to know."

She stares him, mind whirring, is that where she's going wrong? When she's talking to God, she's expecting an answer. Perhaps, humans are so insignificant that no one ever gets a response.

"I mean, if it's you two up against vampires and the like, you need God on your side. How else are you going to survive, let alone achieve anything?"

Sapphire has had enough of the conversation. "Okay, but what are we going to do now?" She can't help the note of irritation that creeps into her voice.

"Personally, I think you might as well get on your knees and pray. You don't stand a fucking chance in hell." There's more than a little challenge in Matt's expression.

"It's here." Jordan's voice cuts through the room.

"What, the vampire?" Matt looks nervously at the window. That's not going to work for me. Never liked the idea of the whole donating blood thing. I refused to go to the doctor's cos it always boils down to them sticking a needle in you."

"For God's sake, Matt. Will you shut up?" Sapphire has a ridiculous urge to laugh again that can only be nerves. "We could make another run for it."

Jordan shakes his head. "We can't keep running."

Matt folds his arms, altering his stance so that his legs are wide apart. "And go fucking where? If any of us had anywhere to go, we wouldn't be in this hellhole."

The two boys stare at each other with shared understanding. Sapphire thinks it would be a beautiful moment if they weren't about to be slaughtered.

12

J ordan stumbles back from the window as the glass shatters inwards. Downstairs, a woman screams.

Everything happens so fast and in slow motion at the same time, which can only be his mind trying to make sense of the situation. His mouth falls open and his eyes fill with tears. He is frozen to the spot.

A black hole fills the space where the window had been. It flows over the sill. Light is sucked inside and the entire room dims until Jordan is convinced there's something wrong with his sight. Thin black tendrils reach for him.

The horror of being touched by the inky blackness makes him stagger away. Only for the nearest few tendrils to shoot out. They are too fast to avoid and before he can escape, they latch onto his thighs and wrists, going on to crawl over his body. The dark lines make it look as though he has cracks opening in his skin.

Jordan frantically bats at them, but the effort is in vain. The tendrils spread and start to tighten wherever they touch. A stinging pain makes him cry out.

The sound spurs the tendrils on and they tighten around his legs. He's jerked into the air. His whole-body shudders as blood rushes to his head. Hanging upside down, he dangles above the carpeted floor. Close by, Sapphire shouts, but he can't concentrate on her words. If he doesn't get the darkness off him, he knows deep down, he's as good as dead. Never has he been so desperate for help.

The room darkens again, but this time it changes.

A single lightbulb swings from the ceiling, making Jordan think he's on a ship. It's the familiar stench that tells him where he is; although it's difficult to believe that a memory can be so real. Every sense is immersed in reliving the night his mother died. One psychologist had warned him this might happen if he continued to repress his childhood.

He automatically seeks out Chantelle. There she is, across the room, smaller than he remembers. There are other people present, but he cannot focus on them.

Most of the luminescence is around him and whatever holds him in its grasp. He cannot see what the creature looks like and doesn't think he saw it that night, so there's no memory to relive.

Mum is thin and pale with wild hair, her face is mostly in shadow, except for when the bulb swings in her direction. Then the light is unkind, highlighting dark rings around her wide eyes. Her mouth is parted in an expression of slack-jawed terror as she stares straight at him.

Jordan is no more grounded in this world than the other, but at least he's upright. His feet dangle a few feet off the dirty brown carpet as a flood of memory overwhelms him all at once. The babyfaces of his brothers and sister appear before his eyes. Flashes of this house, which they'd shared for most of their childhood until this night.

A deep voice says, "Maggie has to pay the price for killing my servant."

The words reverberate through Jordan's little body, not making any sense. Right after that, he is shaken like one of Bronson-dog's indestructible toys. His mother stuffs a hand in her mouth to keep from crying out, and he wants to tell her it's alright but can't when he knows what happens. Even now, he cannot save her, because he's still far too small and weak. The truth is, no matter how big or strong he gets, it's too late.

Jordan doesn't struggle, remembering how he'd tried that earlier. The force holding him is as powerful as God. All he can do is wait for a chance. There's nothing in his head except getting to his mother, because he has to try to change the outcome, never mind the futility.

The deep voice booms, "This one's interesting. Too bad, he has to die."

The creature is playing with him, and it's safest to play dead. Jordan doesn't know where that knowledge comes from, some primal part perhaps.

In the next second, he falls. Consumed with getting to his mother, he manages to get both legs under him. As soon as he touches the floor, he races to her. She's moving to intercept him and they clash. Jordan is pulled into her body. There's a brief lungful of her sweet perfume mixed with the cigarettes he only now remembers she smoked. Her warm arms and bony body crush him. Then, a golden light snatches him up and away.

Jordan yells, knowing that's the last time he will ever see

his mother. She will die in that dingy room that was always too dark, exactly as his monstrous father liked it.

Kassi killed Dene, his father. Jordan remembers she was there the night Chantelle died. She'd been as helpless as him but somehow, like him, she had survived.

Pain brings him back to the present. A searing heat in his ankle and side that makes him want to throw up.

In desperation, he punches at the centre of the darkness. Little fists sink into something with the consistency of dough. He's as small and weak as in the memory and for some reason that thought makes him angry.

The tendrils haven't stopped at his legs, they encircle his chest and have reached his throat. Face hot and eyes bulging, he struggles to drag air into his lungs. Just like back in that room, he is a gnat fighting against an enormous power.

Sapphire shouts something he can't make out for the rushing sound. She seems so far away, even though they are still in his bedroom. It's hard to think beyond the pain. Unable to fight any longer, he goes limp, giving in to the blinding pain.

13

───────

Sapphire has seen a lot of strangeness in her life but the sight of Jordan floating above the bed, punching and kicking the air while being strangled has to be the weirdest. When he starts to drift towards the window, she acts, woken by the fear that he is going to fall to his death on the concrete below.

God wouldn't want her to use magic, but she has to do something. Grabbing a chair, she hardly notices the weight as she runs at the shimmering centre. Halfway there, Sapphire hears the priest in her head.

You will often be tempted. That is what it means to be human. There will come a time when you will believe that you don't have a choice. It is important to remember that you always have a choice and that is part of the test. Stay strong and send the devil packing.

Thinking of that priest, she swings the chair with fury. Before it connects with anything, she's yanked backwards.

"That isn't going to do anything," Matt hisses in her right ear. "You're just going to get yourself killed."

He sounds so calm that she's tempted to smash the chair over his head. It doesn't help that he's right, but she has to do something. The other option is to go against everything she believes in. All the things that have kept her sane her entire childhood.

Matt's earlier words ring in her head; I never expected God to answer. What if all they can do is help each other? How will she live with herself, knowing she could have saved Jordan? The boy has already lost his mother, and he stuck by her despite being hunted by a fucking vampire of all things. Just because it was the right thing to do.

At the moment, she can't do anything with Matt's hands still on her waist. He's too strong to fight, and she's not sure what he intends to do now he's rescued her from imminent death. What's certain is after the entity has finished with Jordan, it will come after them. Slowly, it sinks in that there is only one thing Sapphire can do, because not to act would be the greater evil.

There's no rage driving the act this time. It's less an accident and more a conscious decision to do what needs to be done.

Magic leaves her body in one long rush and she's vaguely aware of Matt letting go and falling away. Heat sears both hands as energy surges through her. It's as if she has stored up years' worth of power that she's releasing in one long continuous stream, despite her earlier attack on the vampire.

She's clumsy and unpractised, barely managing to aim at the centre of the shimmering light. Like firing a gun, she does not feel any impact from the blast once it's left her body. She holds her breath, waiting for something to happen.

Jordan crashes to the floor, but the shimmering light brightens. There's no scream or sign that the entity is in pain. It isn't a living creature, but there should be something. Her attack hasn't done anything except possibly make the thing mad. She sinks to the floor. How could she have given up her principles for nothing? They are going to die and right after she will go to hell.

Sapphire has never questioned her ability before. Now that she thinks about it, there's no proof she's as powerful as they say. All this time, she's been hiding behind religion and the belief that God wouldn't want her to do it, when the truth is, she's afraid of not being as good as everyone thinks. She laughs bitterly, it's hardly surprising since her worth is so wrapped up in her ability. It's always been easier not to try, and it turns out that she was right to be scared because she's a fraud.

Jordan's croaky voice cuts through her spiralling misery, "You need to hit it in the centre."

She's glad he's still alive, but what's he on about? That's precisely what she has just done. She turns to see him raised on his elbows, pointing with eyes fixed on a spot above and to the right of where she'd fired the magic.

"You hit the edges of the black tendrils, hardly causing any damage."

Black tendrils? She cannot see anything black, there's just shimmering light. Is it possible that the problem isn't that her magic is too weak, but rather she cannot see? All that shimmering acts as a mask that stops her from seeing what's happening behind.

Jordan jabs a finger. "Shoot navitas there."

Navitas, the word bounces around her brain, alien and yet right. It removes the mystery and makes magic real, turning it into another tool to be used. The priest didn't condemn her for using navitas. She can do this. There's no time for thinking if she's going to risk hell to save Jordan and Matt.

"Keep pointing."

Jordan does, his face creased in concentration. His arm trembles as he follows something only he can see.

Sapphire used a lot of navitas in the first blast and senses that she doesn't have that much more left, but she has got this. She's so intent on what they have to do that she doesn't notice Matt move until he blocks her view of the shimmering air. He is enormous, standing above both Jordan and her. The worst thing is that he has his back to the entity as if it's safe.

"Matt move, don't turn your back on it." She cranes her head to see around him. "What?"

"You've used your magic. It's over, why don't you give up and join the coven now?"

Her mouth drops open. "How?"

"Don't worry, you aren't going mad. I was sent to keep an eye on Jordan and monitor his potential. It was a bonus when he brought you back here."

Jordan collapses onto his side, not looking at Matt but at a spot over his shoulder. His breathing is noisy, and she nearly jumps out of her skin as his hand squeezes her calf. Understanding hits her, he only appears to have given up. She needs to be ready.

"The coven got in touch when they identified Jordan and the rest you know." He turns to see the shimmer. "There's no need to make this difficult —"

Jordan lifts himself up, his hand shooting out with one

finger pointing at the spot. His whole-body shakes with the effort to hold his torso up.

Sapphire doesn't hesitate. Navitas blasts from her, sending Matt flying into the wardrobe.

The world blurs, shimmering light flying out like droplets when a swimmer dives into a pool. A high-pitched shriek fills the room, only to be cut off half a second later. It's followed by silence, except for the rattle of coat hangers as Matt stirs in the remnants of the broken wardrobe.

Sapphire stands ready to blast him if necessary. They haven't survived the coven for him to cause trouble now.

14

Carpet fibres prickle Jordan's left cheek. When did he last vacuum? From this angle, it must have been long ago. At least there are no tendrils of darkness from this position. Sapphire must have hit the thing dead centre.

He raises his head. Matt is sprawled amongst Jordan's few clothes. On one level, the revelation that Matt has been watching him all this time is shocking. Jordan never dreamed he was important enough for that sort of attention. Another part isn't surprised, his mother made it clear that he needed to hide what he saw. What she meant was, he should hide what he is, he's always known his father isn't completely human.

He pushes himself into a sitting position. Sapphire is standing next to him with wild hair and wide eyes but appearing unhurt.

She turns to him. "I got it...them...whatever it was."

"What do you think it was?"

"I don't know, something the coven made. Whether destroying it hurt them or not, I can't say."

Jordan takes a deep breath and scans what's left of the room. "You did it." It's slowly dawning on him that they can't stay here. "Where now?"

"We should check on the woman downstairs."

Jordan is confused for second and then remembers Elsa screaming. He'd forgotten with everything that's happened. He gets up, groaning as everything in his body protests at the movement, and it takes a few steps to be confident he can walk.

Sapphire hasn't moved. "What if it's the vampire?"

Jordan stops, he hadn't thought of that. Hadn't thought of much but now his mind provides lots of unhelpful pictures of what could have happened while they were fighting the coven. They still have to check.

Why does it have to be a creature from his worst nightmare? Flashes of pale skin drained of blood. His mother lying on a brown carpet, eyes cold and blank. He hadn't seen her killed but his mind is capable of producing vivid graphic images regardless. Of all the creatures, vampires are at the top of the list for inducing the most fear.

Sapphire and Jordan stumble downstairs into a quiet corridor. They share a look of trepidation before moving down the hall to the staff office. There is no sign of Elsa, and Jordan doesn't know whether to be relieved or more concerned. He supposes she could have run away but it seems unlikely.

Sapphire takes a step back, pointing to a smear on the office doorframe. When he looks closer, the dark smudge becomes a bloody handprint. He shudders. That's all the proof he needs that they are dealing with a vampire.

There's no point treading carefully when it'll have super-human hearing. Wherever it's hiding, it knows where they are. How can they come up with a plan when they don't have any resources? There is Sapphire's power, if she's willing to use it, and she might be able to think of something they could do.

Jordan glances at where she's hanging back in the corridor but isn't sure how to ask. "Would you be willing —"

"I'll blast him to hell and back." The words would have been more forceful if her voice hadn't wobbled at the end.

There's a shout from the direction of the stairs. Jordan turns to see a blur of movement behind Sapphire. Without hesitation, he grabs her arm and yanks her into the office. She stumbles into him and they both fall against the far wall.

Matt races down the narrow corridor towards them. A vampire materialises, blocking the way. Jordan gasps, the creature must move too fast to see, which is why it's as though he's come from nowhere. It's the vampire from the pub cellar, only instead of an expensive suit, he's in ill-fitting jeans and a t-shirt.

Matt slows, uncertainty on his face. "I'm with the coven. They —"

Blood sprays across the ceiling, dripping down the cream wall. Matt blinks once and topples forward. Jordan's only coherent thought is that this is how it must have been for his mother. So fast that she didn't even know she was dead. Matt doesn't hit the floor because the vampire catches him and drapes the limp body over one arm like a fashion accessory.

It happens so fast Jordan struggles to make sense of what's happening. Now the vampire turns to look at them.

Trapped in the open office, Jordan knows that there's nowhere they can run. He is not going to die without fighting, like Matt.

Sapphire's voice is loud in his right ear. "Wait." She holds up a hand as if that'll stop him. "Dalton, how much is Madison paying you? Whatever it is, it isn't enough to lose your long life." Jordan is impressed with her confident delivery.

Dalton pauses, grinning. "This is what I do. It's pure fun hunting humans."

"You weren't sent to kill me." Sapphire takes a tiny step forward.

Dalton lets Matt's body fall with a thump. "No." He takes his time answering, "I wouldn't want to upset the coven. They would make a powerful enemy, but he's fair game." He nods at Jordan, grinning as Jordan's body jerks in response to the attention.

"The coven won. I'm going to use my magic now." Sapphire dares to meet his eyes, and there's no doubt in Jordan's mind that she's willing to use her magic. "I stopped them, might even have destroyed them. How easy do you think it's going to be for me to kill you?"

The vampire is suddenly closer. "If that's true, why haven't you done it already?"

Like Dalton, Jordan suspects Sapphire lacks the strength or ability. It might be different if she'd trained. Still, the conversation is giving them time and each second of life is priceless.

The vampire's dark eyes shine. All his focus is on Sapphire. Jordan understands that he is beneath his notice. Sapphire's bluff isn't going to work since even Jordan can see through it.

There has to be another way. He's frozen, knowing instinctively that any movement will alert the vampire, reminding him of Jordan's presence and how expendable he is. Still, he has to do something, has to make his brain work.

He scans the part of the room he can see without moving his head. There's nothing useful. A notice board, stapler and computer, nothing that could be made into a weapon. Of its own volition, his right-hand slides into the pocket of his jeans, closing around the metal disc.

Kassi never told him what it was for, and he isn't even one hundred percent certain it's from her. Desperation is the only thing making him believe that it's worth a try. They have nothing to lose and are going to die as soon as the vampire is sure that Sapphire cannot harm him. How foolish will Jordan feel when they die without trying everything?

"I don't like killing," Sapphire bravely looks into those black eyes. "I was hoping there'd be another way, what do you think?"

Jordan takes that moment to pull the disc out and holds it up, in front of him. "If you will let us go, I will give you this."

The vampire starts to laugh and Jordan realises that he thinks it's a cross. Perhaps he's used to people shoving crosses in his face, along with a prayer. Then, Dalton's eyes narrow and before Jordan can do retract his offer, the disc is snatches from him. He brings it close to his face without making him combust or scream in terror like Jordan hoped.

"Where did you get this, boy?" The humour has gone, leaving a threatening tone.

"A friend gave it to me." Jordan is proud when his voice remains steady. "She —"

"She. This does not belong to a woman."

Jordan has no idea where he finds the strength to speak. "Kassi gave it to me." He is now certain that she did, because who else would have left the disc with Dolores? "She is my friend."

Aloud it sounds pathetic, but the effect on the vampire is astonishing. Dalton stumbles back, while holding out the disc in front of him. Jordan reluctantly reaches out a hand and the vampire drops it into his palm. He's expecting a trick, for the vampire to grab hold and do whatever he did to Matt, but that's not what happens. The disc lands in the centre of Jordan's palm and his fingers automatically close around it. Without another word, the vampire is gone.

15

———

Sapphire stares at Jordan, her eyes a little dazed. "You could have done that earlier."

"I didn't know. I mean who would have thought?" He shakes his head. "Do you really think it's gone?"

"Let's hope so, it must be very scared of your friend." Then, she indicates Matt's body, lying limp on the floor. "Do you think he tried to save us at the end?"

Jordan blinks, not wanting to take his eyes from the disc as if it's going to tell its secret. "I guess we'll never know," he finally looks up, "but, we need to get out of here. I don't want to be interviewed by the police."

"The bastard coven will clear everything up. They won't want to leave a trail of corpses in case they get found out."

Jordan is distracted by the disc again, but manages to say, "If they are still alive."

The light isn't drawn to it and there's no power to the object. A mundane metal disc, nothing to be afraid of, just a large metal coin. Except, going on the vampire's reaction the symbol represents something or someone.

"Sadly, they are, I would know if not, which means they are going to come after us again." Sapphire steps over Matt's body. "Is there anything you desperately need?" Despite the question, she's already heading towards the exit.

He thinks about it. There's his old laptop but it bulky and heavy. It doesn't have anything important on it. A few clothes, and toiletries but nothing that's worth risking the time it would take to collect. He'd lost his possessions in the many moves since the death of his mother.

"Not really." He follows Sapphire outside. "Why do I ache so much?"

She snorts. "I should imagine being strangled by a supernatural entity causes more pain than you'd expect."

Jordan thinks she's right. It doesn't help that there's no hiding from his past now. The good and the bad is all mixed up together as bright and shiny as yesterday.

"Where are we going?" Sapphire is standing on the street, looking left and right as if lost.

Jordan relives the horror on the vampire's face when he recognised the image on the disc. Then, he knows where they need to go and what they need to do. There are no problems seeing a way forward. In fact, his mind is strangely clear.

His eyes connect with Sapphire's pale blue ones. "The person who left this disc for me might help us. All we need to do is find her."

"Is she a powerful witch, because to defeat the coven, she'd have to be badass?"

Jordan smiles, anticipating Sapphire's reaction. "No, she's a demon."

Sapphire's mouth drops open before she whistles. "That explains the vamp's reaction." Smiling, she adds, "Good enough, the coven will think twice before taking on a demon." Her smile fades. "How are we going to find her?"

Jordan sets off toward the bus stop, arms swinging. "By speaking to Dolores who gave me the disc." He glances over his shoulder at her. "She always has the answers but getting her to share them; that will be the hard part." Eyes ahead, he adds, "Then, once we've got this sorted, I'd like to track down my brothers and sister and make sure they're okay."

Sapphire catches him up, linking an arm through his. They have nothing but for the first time since his life was ripped apart, Jordan is filled with purpose. Everything is going to be fine.

AUTHOR NOTES

Thank you for taking a chance on a new author and reading this novella. You cannot imagine how grateful I am. This is the first of many books in the Barathrum Series.

As I'm writing these author notes on the 13 March 2019, there is a full-length novel with an editor, and the second is well on its way to being finished. It's taken a long time to get here. I've had so much to learn about the structure and craft of writing, and I'm *still* learning. None of it matters because the best thing about writing, is writing. I will be writing, even if nobody is reading.

If you are interested in finding out more and would like to sign up to my mailing list, you can find me at www.lucindpebre.com Or, if you want to hear my Yorkshire accent, my friend Anna Singh and I have a podcast at www.divingintowriting.com Thank you, Anna for proof reading yet again!

Stories have always happened in my head, but it's only been in recent years that I have tried to capture them.

My first experience of publishing was thanks to Michael

Anderle. I had a wonderful time writing fan fiction in his Kurtherian Universe. And I got paid! Don't tell him that I would have done it for free. In fact, it was such a great experience that I followed it up by writing more fan fiction in Martha Carr's Oriceran Universe.

What special worlds they are, full of supportive and positive individuals that want the best for each other. I couldn't have found a better place to start out. So, I can't say it enough times; thank you to each and every one of you who has read my work and helped me to become a better author.

If you haven't discovered the Kurtherian and Oriceran Universes yet, have a look, you won't be disappointed. There's also the opportunity to have a go at writing fan fiction, having it published and getting paid!

Just a note about the dedication in the beginning. While writing this book, one of my dogs passed over Rainbow Bridge. He wiggled his way into my heart and I'm hanging onto the piece he left behind. You never know, he might turn up in a novel.

Keep on reading and see you soon,

Lucinda Pebre

www.ingramcontent.com/pod-product-compliance
Lightning Source LLC
Chambersburg PA
CBHW071950190726
48293CB00004B/1420